The Mitten

A Ukrainian Folktale
adapted and illustrated by

JAN BRETT

G. P. Putnam's Sons

An Imprint of Penguin Group (USA)

*For Sylvia Kyle, Ruth Ann Johnson,
Rebecca Lim and Tad Beagley*

*With special thanks to my Ukrainian friend,
Oksana Piaseckyj*

G. P. PUTNAM'S SONS
an imprint of Penguin Random House LLC
375 Hudson Street
New York, NY 10014

Copyright © 1989 by Jan Brett.

G. P. Putnam's Sons is a registered trademark of Penguin Random House LLC.

Library of Congress Cataloging-in-Publication Data
Brett, Jan, 1949–
The mitten : a Ukrainian folktale / adapted and illustrated by Jan Brett.
p. cm. Summary: Several animals sleep snugly in Nicki's lost mitten until the bear sneezes.
[1. Folklore—Ukraine. 2. Mittens—Folklore.] I. Title.
PZ8.1.B755 Mi 1989   398.2'094'771   88-32198

Manufactured in China.
ISBN 978-0-399-25296-9
17 19 20 18 16

Airbrush backgrounds by Joseph Hearne.
Type design by Gunta Alexander.

Many of the stories I write and illustrate come from my imagination. But others begin with a folktale; *The Mitten* is one of those tales. I found out about it from three teachers who were also good friends. They thought I would like to draw the woodland animals and the snowy scenery of the Ukraine, where the tale comes from. They were so right!

The first thing I did was look for all the versions of the story that I could find. Oksana Piaseckyj, who is of Ukrainian heritage, translated them into English for me. In one telling, animals crawl into an old pot, which breaks into bits when too many animals squeeze in. Another version tells about a hunter who goes back to look for his lost mitten and finds it filled with woodland animals.

I liked the idea of a mitten filled with animals, but I didn't like having a hunter shooting the animals. So I imagined the boy called Nicki dropping the white mitten knitted by Baba, his grandmother, as he walks through the snow, oblivious to all the animals living in the forest.

Once I had the story, I was ready to draw. But first I visited the Ukrainian section of New York City to find out more about their culture—the houses, the clothes, their traditions. At the Ukrainian Museum our guide, Christina, gave me lots of good tips. "Be sure and put a stork's nest on the cottage roof. It brings good luck!" she told me.

I did, and I feel it has brought good luck to me because here I am, twenty years later, still getting wonderful letters from children discovering *The Mitten* for the first time!

Jan Brett

Once there was a boy named Nicki who wanted his new mittens made from wool as white as snow.

At first, his grandmother, Baba, did not want to knit white mittens.

"If you drop one in the snow," she warned, "you'll never find it."

But Nicki wanted snow-white mittens, and finally Baba made them.

After she finished she said, "When you come home, first I will look to see if you are safe and sound, but then I will look to see if you still have your snow-white mittens."

So off Nicki went. And it wasn't long until one of his new mittens dropped in the snow and was left behind.

A mole, tired from tunneling along, discovered the mitten and burrowed inside. It was cozy and warm and just the right size, so he decided to stay.

A snowshoe rabbit came hopping by. He stopped for a moment to admire his winter coat. It was then that he saw the mitten, and he wiggled in, feet first. The mole didn't think there was room for both of them, but when he saw the rabbit's big kickers he moved over.

Next a hedgehog came snuffling along. Having spent the day looking under wet leaves for things to eat, he decided to move into the mitten and warm himself. The mole and the rabbit were bumped and jostled, but not being ones to argue with someone covered with prickles, they made room.

As soon as the hedgehog disappeared into the mitten, a big owl, attracted by the commotion, swooped down. When he decided to move in also, the mole, the rabbit, and the hedgehog grumbled. But when they saw the owl's glinty talons, they quickly let him in.

Up through the snow appeared a badger. He eyed the mitten and began to climb in. The mole, the rabbit, the hedgehog, and the owl were not pleased. There was no room left, but when they saw his diggers, they gave him the thumb.

It started snowing, but the animals were snug in the mitten. A waft of warm steam rose in the air, and a fox trotting by stopped to investigate. Just the sight of the cozy mitten made him feel drowsy. The fox poked his muzzle in. When the mole, the rabbit, the hedgehog, the owl, and the badger saw his shiny teeth, they gave the fox lots of room.

A great bear lumbered by. He spied the mitten all plumped up. Not being one to be left out in the cold, he began to nose his way in. The animals were packed in as tightly as could be. But what animal would argue with a bear?

The mitten swelled and stretched. It was pulled and bulged to many times its size. But Baba's good knitting held fast.

Along came a meadow mouse, no bigger than an acorn. She wriggled into the one space left, and made herself comfortable on top of the great bear's nose.

The bear, tickled by the mouse's whiskers, gave an enormous sneeze.

Aaaaa-aaaaa-aaaaa-ca-chew!

The force of the sneeze shot the mitten up into the sky, and scattered the animals in all directions.

On his way home, Nicki saw a white shape in the distance.
It was the lost mitten silhouetted against the blue sky.

As he ran to catch his snow-white mitten, he saw Baba's face in the window. First she looked to see if he was safe and sound, and then she saw that he still had his new mittens.